Night Watch

by Sharon Fear • illustrated by Len Ebert

MODERN CURRICULUM PRESS
Pearson Learning Group

I love to watch at night.

I see them come.
Opossums come at night.

Opossums eat.
Opossums climb.

Opossums hang at night.

The car! Too bright!
They like the dark better.

They hurry home
before day comes.

Opossums climb on Mom.
Opossums ride everywhere.
I see them climb and ride
everywhere.